Yallery Brown

Other brilliant stories to collect:

Yallery Brown

Retold by
Mick Gowar

Illustrated by
Paul Hess

■ SCHOLASTIC
Home of the Story

This version of the story is based on the music theatre piece, The Songs of Yallery Brown, *music by Glyn Evans and words by Mick Gowar, which was commissioned by the Britten Sinfonia and was first performed at the Corn Exchange, Cambridge, as part of the Cambridge City Council's Children's Festival, 1995.*

Scholastic Children's Books,
Commonwealth House, 1–19 New Oxford Street,
London WC1A 1NU, UK
a division of Scholastic Ltd
London ~ New York ~ Toronto ~ Sydney ~ Auckland
Mexico City ~ New Delhi ~ Hong Kong

First published by Scholastic Ltd, 2000

Text copyright © Mick Gowar, 2000
Illustrations copyright © Paul Hess, 2000

ISBN 0 439 01483 2

Printed by Cox and Wyman Ltd, Reading, Berks.

2 4 6 8 10 9 7 5 3 1

The right of Mick Gowar and Paul Hess to be identified as the author
and illustrator respectively of this work has been asserted by them in
accordance with the Copyright, Designs and Patents Act, 1988.

What I'm about to tell you happened on a farm in Suffolk a long time ago. It was a time before modern farm machinery — tractors, combine harvesters and such — when all the work was done by men and horses. It was backbreaking work that began at dawn and didn't cease until sunset.

This particular farm was close to a small village. A muddy road ran from the farm down to the village, and this muddy road ran round an ancient wood. It would have been quicker for anyone going from the farm to the village, or the village to the farm, to cut straight through the wood and not go the long way by the muddy road. But no one ever did.

Everyone in the village knew that in the very middle of the wood was an ancient grove, a circle of trees, open to the sky, where the old folk once worshipped. And in the centre

of that clearing was a flat stone slab.

That stone slab, it was said, was the faeries' dancing floor. And from tiny children, all the villagers were taught never to go into the wood; never to go anywhere near the grove and the faeries' dancing floor.

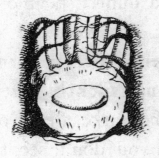

Now, when I say *Faery* I don't mean

the tiny creatures that flit around on silver wings and sleep in flowers and all that nonsense. No. I mean the little dark people that fear all things modern, especially anything made of iron. They came to these islands long before the Romans, long before the Celts. And some people say they're still here. Country people call them Faery folk, and you can sometimes glimpse them out of the corner of your eye, moving silently between the trees, in the darkest part of a wood. Or maybe you don't see them, you just sense them. You can feel the hair

on the back of your neck rise and you know someone is behind you, watching you, and you don't want to look round.

Tom was a boy of sixteen who worked at the farm by the wood. Tom's mother lived in the village, but because his working hours were so long, Tom lived on the farm with all the other lads.

And he worked every day from dawn till sunset, grooming the huge horses that pulled the ploughs and the carts, unblocking the drains and ditches that kept the wet land dry enough to farm, and mending the broken fences.

It was hard, horrible work and Tom hated every minute of it. The only day of the week that Tom didn't dread was

Sunday. That was the only day he had off, and it was the day when he went to the village to visit his mother and she would cook him a lovely Sunday lunch.

One Sunday Tom went to his mother's cottage, and as usual she had cooked a delicious meal of mutton and vegetable stew with a big steamed suet pudding to follow. After lunch they both sat down to rest in the chairs each side of the chimney breast, and they both fell fast asleep. Tom was so tired after a hard week's work that he didn't wake up until he heard the

church bells ringing to call the villagers to Evensong.

"Oh, no!" groaned Tom, getting to his feet. "That means it must be nearly six o'clock, and if I'm not back on the farm by six at the very latest, the farmer will hit me with his heavy stick!"

The farmer was a cruel bully, who beat the boys if they were late or their work was done badly.

14

Saying a hurried "good-bye" to his mother, Tom ran out of the door of the cottage and up the lane. Just as he was turning the corner, the bells stopped.

Oh, no! thought Tom. That means it's six, and I'm going to catch it! It's going to take me at least twenty minutes to get back to the farm along the lane. I'll be late for certain, unless ... unless...

He looked across at the dark woods.

Whatever's in the woods can't be worse than the farmer and his big, heavy stick, thought Tom.

Because no one went into the

woods, there were no pathways trodden between the trees. Twisted branches clutched at Tom's sleeves and tugged like small hands at the legs of his trousers as he ran. Thin twigs scratched at his face like sharp nails on little hands. Sweeping the hair out of his eyes as he ran, Tom could see shadows like watching figures between the trees. He ran blindly on until he arrived at the open grove of ancient oak trees at the very heart of the woods. And there, as the stories told, in the middle of the circle of trees was the stone slab.

"Help me! Help me!"

It was a child's voice crying out. Tom stopped and looked around, but there was no sign of anyone.

"Help me! Help me!" cried the child again. Tom realized that the voice was coming from underneath the stone.

"Help me! Please, help me!" begged the tiny voice. "I only lifted up the stone to look underneath, and while I

was looking it slipped and fell on me. It's so dark under here, and I'm so frightened! Won't someone please, *please* help me!"

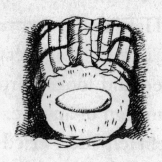

Without a moment's thought poor kind-hearted Tom ran over to the stone slab. He eased his fingers into the soft soil around the slab, and

he heaved with all his strength. He lifted the stone slab just enough to let out ...

... a little wizened, foul-smelling gnome-like creature who blinked at the light and rubbed his eyes. Then the creature let out a loud, cackling laugh and began to sing:

"Brown, Brown,
Yellow and Brown –
I'm Yallery Brown!"

And he was – his skin was a sickly pale yellow, like the skin of a

corpse that's been buried and then dug up again; and his hair was brown and matted with filth so it hung around him like a mouldering shroud. He danced around Tom, and as he danced he sang another song:

"Work as you will, you'll never do well!
Work as you might, you'll never get nowt!
For harm and bad luck and Yallery Brown —
You've let out yourself from under the
   stone!"

That song alone should have made Tom take to his heels and run as fast as he could out of the woods. But Tom was so astonished that he just stood there gawping like a great booby.

"Tom, my boy, you've done me a great service," said Yallery Brown, when he'd tired of dancing and singing. "I've been under that stone

for two hundred years, and now you've let me out. And I'm grateful, Tom, very grateful. You've done me a good turn, Tom, so I'll do you one in return. I'll grant you a wish – yes, anything you want, Tom. You only have to wish for it and it's yours!"

Tom couldn't think of anything to wish for – or rather, he could think of lots of things but couldn't decide on just one.

"Don't be shy, Tom," said Yallery Brown. "Just tell me what you want most, and it's yours!"

But Tom still didn't answer.

"How would you like to be rich, Tom?" asked Yallery Brown. "Sacks and sacks of gold coins, Tom? More money than you've ever dreamed of? You could have more money than the old squire, Tom! Is that what you'd like, Tom? Is it?"

Tom thought hard. He tried to imagine sacks and sacks of money, all of it his. Then he thought about the old squire. The squire had money all right, sacks and sacks of it, but it did him no good. He was so terrified that someone would come and steal his money that he sat up every night, in his nightgown and his cap, with a loaded shotgun in his hands, guarding his money. He never slept and he never had a moment's peace. All that money, thought Tom, and he's the most miserable wretch in the whole county!

"No," said Tom slowly. "No, I don't think I'd want that."

"Well then, how would you like a pretty young wife, Tom?" suggested Yallery Brown with a nudge and a wink. "Just say the word and I can make the prettiest girl in the whole village fall head over heels in love with you. Think of your friend Jack,

who married last Whitsuntide. Wouldn't you like to be as happy as him, Tom?"

But the thought of his friend Jack made Tom stop and think a little longer. Jack and Lucy had been all lovey-dovey and kissy-kissy at first, but not any longer. Now, when Jack came home from the fields, Lucy would be waiting for him to nag him into planting turnips in the garden of their cottage, or to mend the cottage gate, or to clean out the pig they kept. Poor Jack! He never stopped working.

"No," said Tom slowly. "I don't think I'd like that – there'd be too much work to do if I had a wife."

"So you don't like work, Tom?" said sly old Yallery Brown, quick as a flash. "Well, that's where I can help. Just say the word, Tom, and I'll do all your work for you. What more could you wish for?"

27

Tom knew at once, that was what he wanted most in all the world; no more work.

"Yes!" cried Tom. "Yes, that's what I want. I wish for you to do all my work."

"Done!" said Yallery Brown.

"Do you really mean it?" asked Tom.

"I certainly do," said Yallery Brown.

"Thank—"

"Stop!" yelled Yallery Brown. "You must never, ever thank me, Tom. You did me a favour, letting me out from under the stone. So I owe you a favour.

That's keeping things in balance, Tom. Your world and my world, they've got to be kept in balance, Tom. If you ever thank me, well, then everything's out of balance again. And you won't ever see me again, Tom, and the worst of bad luck will come to you. So remember, Tom, never, ever thank me!"

And Yallery Brown skipped away into the trees singing:

"Work as you will, you'll never do well!
Work as you might, you'll never get nowt!
For harm and bad luck and Yallery Brown —
You've let out yourself from under the
  stone!"

Tom ran all the way through the woods, back to the farm. All the way back he was dreading the beating he was sure to get from the farmer. But when he got back to the farm his luck seemed to have changed already.

The farmer had gone to church, and he hadn't noticed that Tom was late back.

Next morning, Tom was up at dawn as usual. He staggered out of the farmhouse bleary-eyed and yawning, and made his way to the stables to start grooming the great cart horse. But when Tom got to the stall his mouth fell open with astonishment. The horse was groomed till its broad back was gleaming like polished mahogany, and its tail and mane had been plaited with ribbons, as if it were going to the County Show.

Tom ran from the stables down to the ditch at the bottom of the West Field. Unblocking the ditch and mending the fence were his next jobs. But when Tom arrived, the ditch was clear and the fence was so skilfully mended that you couldn't tell which part had fallen down.

"Yallery Brown!" Tom shouted in delight.

"Yes?" said a crackly voice behind him.

Tom turned and saw the little shrivelled creature squatting on a fence post.

"Thank—" began Tom.

"*Tom!*" scolded Yallery Brown. "How many times must I tell you – never thank me, or your luck will turn bad!" And shaking his head, and smiling to himself, Yallery Brown skipped away down the field singing:

33

"Work as you will, you'll never do well!
Work as you might, you'll never get nowt!
For harm and bad luck and Yallery Brown —
You've let out yourself from under the
    stone!"

Next day, and the day after, and the day after that, Tom went out to work and found that all his work had been done for him by Yallery Brown. By the

end of the week, Tom didn't even bother to get out of bed any more. He knew his work was done, and done better than he could do it – so why bother to get up?

That's when things started to go badly for the other farm lads. While Tom lay in bed, Yallery Brown did all his work, but he wrecked the work of the other lads as well. While Tom's horse was groomed and gleaming, the horses the other lads had to care for were lame and their coats were smeared with muck. The fences Tom had to mend were perfectly patched, but the

fences the other lads mended collapsed. Tom's drains and ditches were clear, but the other lads' ditches were full of weeds and mud and rubbish.

It didn't take the other lads long to work out what must be happening. Tom lay in bed every day until noon, so someone – or something – was doing all his work and wrecking

theirs. It was *witchcraft*! They knew what to do.

Next morning Tom was woken, at dawn, by a stick hitting him across the shoulders.

"Get up, witch-boy!" shouted a voice.

There was another blow across his back, even harder.

Tom looked up. The other lads were all around his bed. They started chanting: "Witch-boy! Witch-boy!"

Tom jumped out of bed, and the other lads laid into him with their sticks, all freshly cut from the rowan tree which

grew at the top of West Field.

Tom tried to run from the room, holding his arms over his head to keep the blows off him. The farmlads drove him down the stairs, out of the farmhouse, across the farmyard, and out of the gate and into the lane.

"Stop!" pleaded Tom. "It wasn't me —"

But the lads kept beating him with their sticks and chanting: "Witch-boy! Witch-boy!"

Tom ran down the lane, with the lads after him. "Run, witch-boy," they shouted, "and never come back!"

Tom ran until he came to the turn at the top of the lane. But the lads were still close behind, waving their sticks and shouting: "Away with you, witch-boy, or we'll hang you from the old gibbet at the crossroads!"

Desperately, Tom plunged into the woods.

The lads stopped. They weren't

going to follow him into the woods.
Every one of them knew that evil lurked
in the woods. So much the better if
Tom came to a bad end in the woods,
they all agreed. Breathing deeply, but
satisfied with their morning's work, the
farm lads shouldered their sticks and
began to walk slowly back to the farm.

Tom fled on through the trees,

blinded by his tears and the blood which flowed from a large gash on his forehead. Hawthorn twigs whipped into his eyes and gouged his cheeks, but Tom plunged on through the thickest part of the wood until he reached the clearing. Tom fell to the ground, sobbing with pain. He gulped air into his lungs, and as his breath returned he sat up.

He knew who was to blame, and he knew what he had to do.

"Yallery Brown!" he called. "Yallery Brown – I want a word with you!"

"Here I am, Tom," said a hoarse

voice behind him. "Oh dear, Tom! You do look a state!" And the little creature began to laugh.

"It's all your fault!" cried Tom. "I wish I'd never met you, Yallery Brown, and I'll thank you never to help me ever again!"

There was a sudden silence in the wood. Even the birds stopped their

twittering.

"What did you say?" asked Yallery Brown, very quiet and menacing.

"I said: *I'll thank you never to help me ever again*," Tom repeated.

"Oh dear, Tom," said Yallery Brown. "I warned you never to thank me, and now you have. I must go, and you'll never see me again, Tom. But someone will come in my place, Tom, and you'll wish they hadn't.

"By thanking me, Tom, you've set me free. That means the balance is gone between our two worlds. I'm free, but now there's an empty place

beneath the stone. I must go now, Tom, but listen – *they* are coming!"

Tom listened, but all he could hear was a rustling, like the wind in the dry leaves. No, wait a moment. Tom strained his ears. Now it sounded more like tiny footsteps.

Tom tried to stand up, but tiny fingers clutched at his arms and legs,

pinning him to the ground. Tom tried to pull away, but the tiny hands were too many and too strong. Slowly, slowly Tom was dragged backwards across the forest floor towards the old stone slab. Turning his head, Tom saw the stone slab was raised up. He let out a piercing cry as the tiny hands dragged him beneath the stone. His scream was cut off as the terrible darkness crashed down on top of him.

In the centre of an old dark wood, in an ancient grove where the old folk once worshipped, lies a grey stone

slab. Anyone standing in that grove would hear a small voice, like a child's voice, crying:

"Help me! Please, help me! I only lifted up the stone to look underneath, and while I was looking it slipped and fell on me. It's so dark under here, and I'm so frightened! Won't someone please, please help me!"

It is the voice of a creature that has

been under that stone for many years, crying to be let out. But no one ever goes into the wood, and no one hears the voice. It is better that the creature stays beneath the stone crying and wailing. For if it's ever let out, the balance between the worlds would be disturbed once again – and who knows what would happen then?

Work as you will, you'll never do well!
Work as you might, you'll never get nowt!
For harm and bad luck and Yallery Brown –
You've let out yourself from under the stone!